.CLASSICS.
Illustrated®

Alexandre Dumas
THE THREE MUSKETEERS

essay by
Sherwood Smith, M.A.

ACCLAIM BOOKS
STUDY GUIDE

The Three Musketeers

art by George Evans
cover by John Paul Leon

For Classics Illustrated Study Guides
computer recoloring by VanHook Studios
editor: Madeleine Robins
assistant editor: Gregg Sanderson
design: Scott Friedlander

Dale-Chall R.L.: 7.2

ISBN 1-57840-029-5

Acclaim Books, New York, NY
Printed in the United States

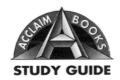

STUDY GUIDE

THE THREE MUSKETEERS

Alexandre Dumas

ON AN APRIL DAY IN 1625, D'ARTAGNAN, A YOUNG MAN FROM GASCONY, RODE TO PARIS ON AN ANCIENT YELLOW HORSE TO SEEK HIS FORTUNE. IN HIS POCKET WERE 15 CROWNS AND A LETTER OF INTRODUCTION TO MONSIEUR DE TREVILLE, THE CAPTAIN OF THE KING'S MUSKETEERS.

WHEN HE ARRIVED AT MONSIEUR DE TREVILLE'S HOTEL, HE FOUND THE COURT FILLED WITH MUSKETEERS.

HE WAS ADMITTED TO DE TREVILLE'S APARTMENT.

ONE MOMENT, PLEASE, WHILE I FINISH WITH ANOTHER MATTER. ATHOS! PORTHOS! ARAMIS!

THREE MUSKETEERS IMMEDIATELY ENTERED.

I HAVE HEARD, GENTLEMEN, THAT SOME OF THE KING'S MUSKETEERS FOUGHT THE CARDINAL'S GUARDS IN THE RUE FEROU YESTERDAY.

LOUIS XIII AND CARDINAL RICHELIEU HAVE THEIR DIFFERENCES, BUT THIS DOES NOT MEAN MUSKETEERS AND GUARDS ARE FREE TO BRAWL IN THE STREETS.

YOU ARE NOT TO EXPOSE YOUR LIVES NEEDLESSLY IN THIS WAY. THE KING, BESET BY ENEMIES AND INTRIGUES AS HE IS, HAS NEED OF ALL OF HIS MUSKETEERS.

*A*T A SIGN FROM DE TREVILLE, THE THREE MEN WENT OUT, LEAVING D'ARTAGNAN IN THE CHAMBER.

I KNEW YOUR FATHER AND RESPECTED HIM VERY MUCH. WHAT CAN I DO FOR HIS SON?

I WISH MORE THAN ANYTHING TO BE A MUSKETEER.

TO BECOME A MUSKETEER ONE MUST HAVE SERVED TWO YEARS IN SOME OTHER REGIMENT, OR HAVE DISTINGUISHED HIMSELF BY CERTAIN BRILLIANT ACTIONS.

I WILL GET YOU ADMITTED TO THE ROYAL MILITARY ACADEMY. YOU WILL LEARN MUCH THERE. MEANWHILE, FEEL FREE TO CALL UPON ME TO LET ME KNOW HOW YOU ARE DOING.

ELATED, D'ARTAGNAN BOUNDED DOWN THE STAIRS AND COLLIDED WITH ATHOS.

EXCUSE ME.

YOU SAY "EXCUSE ME" AND BELIEVE THAT IS SUFFICIENT? YOUR MANNERS ARE VERY BAD.

IT IS NOT YOU WHO CAN GIVE ME LESSONS IN GOOD MANNERS, I WARN YOU.

LET US MEET NEAR THE CARMES DESCHAUX AT NOON AND SETTLE THIS MATTER.

GOOD. I WILL BE THERE.

D'ARTAGNAN CONTINUED AND AT THE GATE CAME UPON PORTHOS AND A FRIEND.

*A*S HE PUSHED PAST THEM THE WIND BLEW OUT PORTHOS' CLOAK WHICH ENVELOPED D'ARTAGNAN IN ITS FOLDS.

CONFOUND IT, WHAT ARE YOU DOING?

EXCUSE ME, YOUR CLOAK--

YOU MUST BE TAUGHT NOT TO RUN AGAINST MUSKETEERS IN THIS FASHION. I WILL SEE YOU AT ONE O'CLOCK BEHIND THE LUXEMBOURG.

VERY WELL.

D'ARTAGNAN PASSED OUT ONTO THE STREET WHERE HE SOON CAME UPON ARAMIS TALKING TO SOME FRIENDS.

HE HAS DROPPED HIS HANDKERCHIEF AND IS STEPPING ON IT!

I BELIEVE, MONSIEUR, THIS IS A HANDKERCHIEF YOU WOULD BE SORRY TO LOSE.

AH, HA! WILL YOU STILL INSIST YOU ARE NOT FOND OF THE CHARMING LADY WHO GAVE YOU THIS?

THIS HANDKERCHIEF IS NOT MINE!

WHEN ARAMIS'S FRIENDS DEPARTED, HE TURNED ON D'ARTAGNAN.

YOU ARE A FOOL, SIR, IF YOU DO NOT KNOW THAT WHEN PEOPLE TREAD UPON HANDKERCHIEFS IT IS FOR A REASON. LET US MEET AT TWO O'CLOCK AT DE TREVILLE'S HOTEL TO ARRANGE A DUEL.

THOUGHTFULLY, D'ARTAGNAN STARTED FOR HIS FIRST APPOINTMENT.

DECIDEDLY I CANNOT DRAW BACK. BUT AT LEAST IF I AM KILLED, I SHALL BE KILLED BY A MUSKETEER.

HE FOUND ATHOS AT THE APPOINTED SPOT.

I HAVE ASKED TWO OF MY FRIENDS TO BE SECONDS. AH, HERE THEY COME.

BUT I AM TO FIGHT THIS GENTLEMAN!

AND I!

TRUE, BUT MONSIEUR ATHOS HAS FIRST CLAIM ON ME. ON GUARD!

THE TWO MEN HAD JUST CROSSED SWORDS WHEN...

THE CARDINAL'S GUARDS! SHEATHE SWORDS!

HOLA! MUSKETEERS FIGHTING? AND WHAT OF THE LAWS AGAINST DUELING? BE GOOD ENOUGH TO FOLLOW US.

SHALL WE FIGHT? IT IS FIVE AGAINST THREE.

NO, GENTLEMEN. THERE ARE FOUR OF US!

*D*RAWING THEIR SWORDS, D'ARTAGNAN AND THE MUSKETEERS FOUGHT TOGETHER.

*I*N A FEW MINUTES ALL THE GUARDS WERE WOUNDED OR DEAD.

*T*RIUMPHANTLY, THE FOUR FRIENDS WALKED BACK TO DE TREVILLE'S HOTEL.

IF I AM NOT YET A MUSKETEER, AT LEAST I HAVE ENTERED UPON MY APPRENTICESHIP, HAVEN'T I?

D'ARTAGNAN FOUND LODGING IN A MODEST HOUSE AND SPENT A GREAT DEAL OF TIME WITH THE MUSKETEERS. ONE DAY WHEN HE WAS ALONE AT HOME, HIS LANDLORD CAME TO CALL.

AH, MONSIEUR BONACIEUX, WHAT CAN I DO FOR YOU?

I HAVE HEARD YOU SPOKEN OF AS A VERY BRAVE YOUNG MAN, WHICH EMBOLDENS ME TO CONFIDE IN YOU.

IT IS ABOUT CONSTANCE, MY WIFE. SHE HAS BEEN CARRIED OFF!

THE DEVIL! BY WHOM?

I DON'T KNOW, BUT I AM SURE THERE IS SOME INTRIGUE IN THIS. CONSTANCE IS SEAMSTRESS TO THE QUEEN AND IS IN HER CONFIDENCE.

IT IS KNOWN THAT THE QUEEN, ABANDONED BY THE KING AND SPIED UPON BY THE CARDINAL, IS LOVED BY THE ENGLISH DUKE OF BUCKINGHAM. I THINK CONSTANCE IS SOMEHOW CAUGHT UP IN THIS.

I WILL TRY TO THINK WHAT CAN BE DONE FOR HER.

D'ARTAGNAN CONFIDED THE MATTER TO HIS FRIENDS. SEVERAL DAYS LATER...

IT SOUNDS AS IF SOMEONE IS BEING MISTREATED IN MONSIEUR BONACIEUX'S APARTMENT.

HE RUSHED DOWNSTAIRS AND QUICKLY PUT THE MEN TO FLIGHT.

AH, MONSIEUR, YOU HAVE SAVED ME!

ARE YOU MADAME BONACIEUX?

YES. THOSE MEN WERE AGENTS OF THE CARDINAL, FROM WHOM I ESCAPED.

HOW DID YOU DO THAT?

I TOOK ADVANTAGE OF A MOMENT WHEN THEY LEFT ME ALONE, BUT, AS YOU SEE, THEY FOLLOWED ME.

WHAT WILL YOU DO NOW?

GO BACK TO THE QUEEN. BUT FIRST I MUST FIND SOMEONE TO GO ON A MISSION FOR HER MAJESTY.

I WOULD BE DELIGHTED TO SERVE BOTH YOU AND HER, MADAME.

BUT IT WILL BE TERRIBLY DANGEROUS.

ALL THE BETTER.

VERY WELL, THEN. GO TO LONDON AND DELIVER THIS MESSAGE TO THE DUKE OF BUCKINGHAM. IT ASKS THAT HE SEND BACK TWELVE DIAMOND STUDS THE QUEEN GAVE HIM.

YOU SEE, THE CARDINAL SUSPECTS THE QUEEN. HE HAS HAD THE KING INSIST SHE WEAR THESE STUDS AT A BALL NEXT WEEK. IF SHE DOES NOT, ALL IS LOST.

I SHALL GO AT ONCE.

ATHOS, PORTHOS AND ARAMIS INSISTED ON ACCOMPANYING HIM.

ONE MAN IS TOO EASILY DESTROYED BY THE CARDINAL'S SPIES. BUT FOUR MEN, SHOULDER TO SHOULDER, MIGHT SUCCEED.

THAT IS OUR MOTTO, IS IT NOT--ALL FOR ONE, ONE FOR ALL!

ALL FOR ONE, ONE FOR ALL!

THIS IS THE LETTER I MUST DELIVER TO THE DUKE OF BUCKINGHAM. IF I AM KILLED, ONE OF YOU MUST TAKE IT AND RIDE ON. IF HE IS KILLED, A THIRD WILL TAKE HIS PLACE, AND SO ON.

BRAVO, D'ARTAGNAN! LET US LEAVE WITHIN THE HOUR.

THEY WENT AS FAR AS CHANTILLY WHERE THEY ALIGHTED AT AN INN.

IN THE COMMON ROOM THEY FELL INTO CONVERSATION WITH A MAN WHO HAD JUST ARRIVED.

LET US DRINK TO THE CARDINAL.

YES, IF YOU WILL, IN TURN, DRINK TO THE KING.

THERE IS NO OTHER KING BUT THE CARDINAL!

PORTHOS ROSE, AND THE STRANGER DREW HIS SWORD.

KILL THE FELLOW AND REJOIN US AS SOON AS YOU CAN.

*T*HE THREE FRIENDS CONTINUED THEIR JOURNEY. BEFORE LONG THEY CAME TO A GROUP OF MEN WORKING ON THE ROAD.

*T*HE WORKERS SUDDENLY PRODUCED MUSKETS FROM A DITCH AND PEPPERED THEM WITH BULLETS.

AN AMBUSCADE! FORWARD!

*A*RAMIS, THOUGH WOUNDED, CLUNG TO HIS HORSE'S MANE AND ESCAPED WITH THE OTHERS.

*B*UT SOON...

I CAN GO NO FURTHER. LEAVE ME AT THIS INN AND GO ON.

VERY WELL.

D'ARTAGNAN AND ATHOS CONTINUED UNTIL MIDNIGHT, WHEN THEY STOPPED AT AN INN. THE NEXT MORNING ATHOS WENT INTO THE INNKEEPER'S OFFICE TO PAY THE BILL.

THIS MONEY IS COUNTERFEIT. I'LL HAVE YOU AND YOUR COMPANION ARRESTED!

YOU SCOUNDREL! I'LL CUT YOUR EARS OFF!

JUST THEN FOUR MEN RUSHED IN AND FELL UPON ATHOS.

I AM TAKEN! GO ON, D'ARTAGNAN! SPUR! SPUR!

I WOULD LIKE TO CROSS TO ENGLAND IMMEDIATELY.

NOTHING WOULD BE MORE EASY, BUT WE HAD ORDERS THIS MORNING THAT NO ONE BE ALLOWED TO CROSS WITHOUT PERMISSION FROM THE CARDINAL.

I HAVE AN ORDER FROM THE CARDINAL GRANTING ME THAT PERMISSION.

MONSIEUR MUST FIRST HAVE IT CERTIFIED BY THE GOVERNOR OF THE PORT WHO LIVES YONDER.

THE MAN SET OFF TOWARD THE GOVERNOR'S HOUSE, CLOSELY FOLLOWED BY D'ARTAGNAN.

MONSIEUR, A MOMENT, PLEASE.

I BEG YOU TO RENDER ME A SERVICE. I WOULD LIKE THE ORDER YOU ARE BEARING.

YOU ARE JESTING, I PRESUME. LET ME PASS!

YOU SHALL NOT PASS!

THE MAN DREW HIS SWORD AND FELL UPON D'ARTAGNAN.

D'ARTAGNAN WOUNDED HIM SEVERELY AND TOOK THE ORDER FROM HIS POCKET.

HE REACHED LONDON WITHOUT FURTHER DIFFICULTY AND WAS SOON IN THE PRESENCE OF THE DUKE OF BUCKINGHAM.

HAS ANY MISFORTUNE BEFALLEN THE QUEEN?

NO, BUT I BELIEVE SHE IS IN SOME PERIL. HERE IS A MESSAGE FROM HER.

GREAT HEAVENS! I WILL GET THE STUDS IMMEDIATELY.

BUT...

WHAT IS THE MATTER, MILORD?

ALL IS LOST! TWO OF THE STUDS ARE MISSING. THERE ARE BUT TEN OF THEM.

CAN THEY HAVE BEEN STOLEN?

THE ONLY TIME I WORE THESE STUDS WAS AT A BALL LAST WEEK. MILADY DE WINTER STOOD BESIDE ME TALKING FOR QUITE A LONG TIME.

SHE IS AN AGENT OF THE CARDINAL. SHE MUST HAVE TAKEN THEM.

WHAT'S TO BE DONE? THE BALL IS IN FIVE DAYS.

I WILL HAVE TWO MADE EXACTLY LIKE THE OTHERS.

THE DUKE SET HIS JEWELER TO WORK. TWO DAYS LATER, D'ARTAGNAN WAS READY TO RETURN TO FRANCE WITH TWELVE DIAMOND STUDS.

HOW CAN I EVER REPAY MY DEBT TO YOU?

I CONFESS, YOUR GRACE, THAT WITH WAR IMMINENT BETWEEN OUR TWO COUNTRIES, I MUST LOOK UPON YOU AS A FUTURE ENEMY. THAT WHICH I DID, I DID FOR MY QUEEN.

YOUR HAND, YOUNG MAN. PERHAPS WE SHALL SOON MEET ON THE FIELD OF BATTLE, BUT NOW WE PART GOOD FRIENDS, I TRUST.

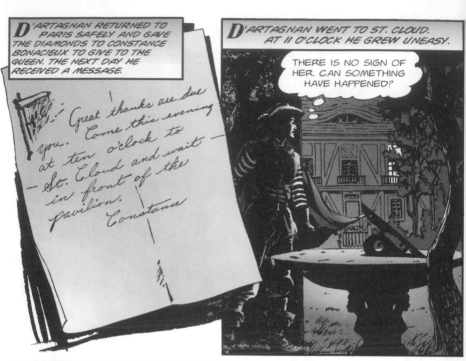

D'ARTAGNAN RETURNED TO PARIS SAFELY AND GAVE THE DIAMONDS TO CONSTANCE BONACIEUX TO GIVE TO THE QUEEN. THE NEXT DAY HE RECEIVED A MESSAGE.

Great thanks are due you. Come this evening at ten o'clock to — St. Cloud and wait — in front of the pavilion.

Constance

D'ARTAGNAN WENT TO ST. CLOUD. AT 11 O'CLOCK HE GREW UNEASY.

THERE IS NO SIGN OF HER. CAN SOMETHING HAVE HAPPENED?

HE SWUNG HIMSELF UP INTO A TREE FROM WHICH HE COULD SEE INTO THE LIGHTED ROOM.

GREAT HEAVENS! SOMEONE MUST HAVE TAKEN HER AWAY BY FORCE!

JUMPING DOWN, D'ARTAGNAN MADE ANOTHER DISCOVERY.

HER GLOVE! TORN AND MUDDY!

D'ARTAGNAN WENT TO DE TREVILLE AND TOLD HIM THE STORY.

THIS ALL SAVORS OF THE CARDINAL. HE MUST KNOW HOW THE DIAMOND STUDS GOT FROM LONDON TO PARIS.

IF I WERE YOU I WOULD LEAVE PARIS AS SOON AS POSSIBLE. THE CARDINAL IS A FORMIDABLE ENEMY, WITH ALL THE DEVIL'S TRICKS AT HIS COMMAND.

BUT I MUST TRY TO FIND CONSTANCE!

THERE IS NOTHING YOU CAN DO. I WILL TELL THE QUEEN WHAT HAS HAPPENED. SHE MAY BE ABLE TO HELP THE YOUNG WOMAN,

IN THAT CASE, I SHALL LEAVE IMMEDIATELY AND SEEK OUT ATHOS, PORTHOS AND ARAMIS.

D'ARTAGNAN WENT TO THE INN WHERE HE HAD PARTED WITH PORTHOS.

CAN YOU TELL ME WHAT HAS HAPPENED TO MY FRIEND WHO WAS DETAINED HERE BY A QUARREL A WEEK AGO?

MONSIEUR PORTHOS? HE IS HERE, RECOVERING FROM A CHEST WOUND. AH, THE BILL HE HAS RUN UP!

D'ARTAGNAN FOUND PORTHOS IN HIS ROOM.

D'ARTAGNAN! YOU ARE WELCOME, MY DEAR FELLOW. DID YOU HEAR MY SORRY STORY? WHEN I WAS FIGHTING WITH THE STRANGER I TRIPPED ON A STONE AND STRAINED MY KNEE.

INDEED?

IT WAS LUCKY FOR THE RASCAL, FOR I SHOULD HAVE LEFT HIM DEAD ON THE SPOT.

AS I SEE YOU ARE WELL PROVIDED FOR, I WILL GO ON TO FIND THE OTHERS. WE WILL CALL FOR YOU ON THE WAY BACK.

HE FOUND ARAMIS AT ANOTHER INN.

IS THIS ARAMIS, OR HAVE I MISTAKEN YOUR ROOM FOR THAT OF A CHURCHMAN?

I HAVE ALWAYS INTENDED TO TAKE THE HOLY ORDERS AND I AM NOW ABOUT TO DO SO.

IN THAT CASE, I SHALL BURN THIS LETTER WHICH CAME FOR YOU IN PARIS.

WHAT LETTER?

OH, ONLY FROM SOME WOMAN, I THINK.

AH, SHE LOVES ME STILL! SHE IS NOT FAITHLESS!

DEAR FRIEND, HAPPINESS STIFLES ME. I RETURN TO THE WORLD.

BECAUSE ARAMIS HAD NOT COMPLETELY RECOVERED FROM HIS WOUNDS, D'ARTAGNAN WENT ON ALONE. HE JOURNEYED UNTIL HE CAME TO THE INN WHERE HE HAD LAST SEEN ATHOS.

YOU ONCE HAD THE AUDACITY TO ACCUSE A GENTLEMAN OF PASSING BAD MONEY. WHAT HAS BECOME OF HIM?

AH, MONSIEUR, HE FOUGHT LIKE A TIGER. AS HE RETREATED HE FOUND THE WAY TO THE CELLAR AND BARRICADED HIMSELF IN IT.

I SEE. YOU MADE HIM YOUR PRISONER.

OH, NO! WE KNOW WE ACCUSED HIM WRONGLY, AND HAVE BEEN TRYING TO GET HIM OUT, BUT HE WILL NOT COME.

ALL OUR SUPPLIES ARE IN THE CELLAR. HE WILL NOT LET US IN AND WE ARE FORCED TO TURN AWAY TRAVELLERS WHO COME FOR FOOD AND DRINK.

OH, MONSIEUR, IF YOU COULD ONLY PERSUADE HIM TO COME OUT! IF HE STAYS IN THE CELLAR ANOTHER WEEK I SHALL BE RUINED!

D'ARTAGNAN WENT TO THE CELLAR.

ATHOS, OPEN THE DOOR.

IS THAT D'ARTAGNAN? WAIT WHILE I UNBAR IT.

YOU HAVE EATEN AND DRUNK WELL, I SEE, DEAR FELLOW.

I AM DEAD DRUNK, I MUST HAVE HAD 150 BOTTLES.

MY WINE, MY WINE! IT IS NEARLY ALL GONE! AND WHERE ARE MY SAUSAGES? I AM A RUINED MAN!

THIS WILL TEACH YOU TO TREAT YOUR GUESTS IN MORE COURTEOUS FASHION.

COME, WE WILL GO TO A ROOM. YOU THINK I AM DRUNK BUT MY IDEAS ARE NEVER SO CLEAR AS WHEN I HAVE HAD PLENTY OF WINE.

I THINK I WILL TELL YOU A STORY OF LOVE. ONE OF MY FRIENDS, A COUNT, FELL IN LOVE WITH A BEAUTIFUL BUT PENNILESS YOUNG GIRL AND MARRIED HER.

"ONE DAY WHEN THEY WERE OUT HUNTING SHE FELL FROM HER HORSE AND FAINTED. HE LOOSENED HER DRESS AND WHAT DO YOU THINK HE FOUND ON HER SHOULDER?"

A FLEUR-DE-LIS! SHE HAD BEEN A THIEF AND WAS BRANDED!

GREAT HEAVENS! WHAT DID HE DO THEN?

HE TIED HER HANDS BEHIND HER BACK AND HANGED HER FROM A TREE!

WHAT A GHASTLY THING TO HAVE HAPPENED TO YOUR FRIEND!

MY FRIEND? D'ARTAGNAN, IT WAS I!

D'ARTAGNAN AND ATHOS SET OUT THE NEXT DAY, STOPPING ON THE WAY FOR ARAMIS AND PORTHOS. SOON THE FOUR FRIENDS WERE AGAIN IN PARIS. ONE DAY WHEN D'ARTAGNAN WAS OUT RIDING HE CAME ACROSS A CARRIAGE DRAWN UP BY THE ROADSIDE.

IN IT WAS A BEAUTIFUL LADY TALKING ANGRILY TO A CAVALIER.

MADAME, I AM MONSIEUR D'ARTAGNAN OF HIS MAJESTY'S GUARDS. MAY I OFFER MY SERVICES?

I SHOULD WELCOME YOUR PROTECTION, WERE NOT THIS GENTLEMAN MY BROTHER-IN-LAW.

MY NAME IS LADY DE WINTER AND I AM STAYING IN THE VILLA YONDER. PERHAPS YOU WILL CALL ON ME.

CAN THIS BE THE MILADY DE WINTER THE DUKE OF BUCKINGHAM SUSPECTED OF STEALING THE QUEEN'S STUDS?

*E*AGER TO LEARN MORE, D'ARTAGNAN ACCEPTED THE INVITATION AND BEGAN TO VISIT MILADY OFTEN. ONE NIGHT HE HEARD HER TALKING TO HER MAID.

IF MADAME HATES MONSIEUR D'ARTAGNAN SO, WHY DOES SHE ENCOURAGE HIM TO CALL?

HE AND I HAVE SOMETHING TO SETTLE THAT HE IS QUITE IGNORANT OF. HE WAS VERY NEAR MAKING ME LOSE MY CREDIT WITH THE CARDINAL OVER TWO DIAMOND STUDS.

MADAME HAS AT LEAST REVENGED HERSELF BY HAVING HIS FRIEND, MADAME BONACIEUX, ABDUCTED.

D'ARTAGNAN FLUNG OPEN THE DOOR.

D'ARTAGNAN!

WHAT HAVE YOU DONE WITH CONSTANCE?

D'ARTAGNAN SEIZED MILADY BY THE SHOULDER. AS SHE PULLED AWAY, THE NECK OF HER GOWN TORE.

GREAT GOD! THE FLEUR-DE-LIS! YOU ARE BRANDED!

YOU WRETCH! YOU KNOW MY SECRET! YOU SHALL DIE!

SHOCKED BY THE WILD AND EVIL LOOK IN HER EYES, D'ARTAGNAN OPENED THE DOOR AND RAN FROM THE HOUSE.

*H*E RACED TO ATHOS' APARTMENT.

HOW PALE YOU ARE, MY FRIEND. WHAT HAS HAPPENED?

I HAVE JUST MET WITH A TERRIBLE ADVENTURE. ATHOS, MILADY IS MARKED WITH THE FLEUR-DE-LIS UPON HER SHOULDER!

ARE YOU SURE THE OTHER WOMAN IS DEAD--THE ONE YOU TOLD ME ABOUT?

IS THIS LADY FAIR, WITH BLUE EYES? IS THE FLEUR-DE-LIS SMALL AND RED IN COLOR?

YES, YES!

THEN SHE MUST SOMEHOW HAVE SET HERSELF FREE TO CONTINUE HER WICKED WAYS.

I FEAR I HAVE INVITED A TERRIBLE VENGEANCE UPON BOTH OF US.

SOON AFTER, THE FOUR FRIENDS LEFT PARIS ON A CAMPAIGN AGAINST THE ENGLISH AT LA ROCHELLE. D'ARTAGNAN, BEING IN ANOTHER COMPANY, WAS SEPARATED FROM THE THREE MUSKETEERS. ONE DAY...

WINE, MONSIEUR--A PRESENT FROM MESSIEURS ATHOS, PORTHOS AND ARAMIS.

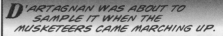

D'ARTAGNAN WAS ABOUT TO SAMPLE IT WHEN THE MUSKETEERS CAME MARCHING UP.

YOU COULD NOT HAVE COME AT A BETTER TIME. I WAS ABOUT TO DRINK THE WINE YOU SENT ME.

BUT WE SENT YOU NO WINE.

WHAT!

THEY HURRY TO D'ARTAGNAN'S ROOM.

HE'S DEAD!

THE WINE WAS POISONED. MILADY MUST HAVE SENT IT.

THIS IS WAR TO THE DEATH. TAKE CARE OF YOURSELF UNTIL WE MEET AGAIN.

THE THREE MUSKETEERS RETURNED TO THEIR CAMP. ONE NIGHT THEY WERE RIDING TOGETHER WHEN THEY HEARD THE SOUND OF HORSES.

WHO GOES THERE? ANSWER OR WE CHARGE.

BEWARE OF WHAT YOU ARE ABOUT TO DO, GENTLEMEN. WHO ARE YOU?

KING'S MUSKETEERS. AND YOU?

CARDINAL RICHELIEU.

YOUR PARDON, MONSEIGNEUR. WE DID NOT KNOW YOU.

I REQUEST YOU GENTLEMEN TO FOLLOW ME AND BE MY ESCORT FOR THE EVENING.

THE MUSKETEERS ACCOMPANIED THE CARDINAL TO AN INN.

WAIT FOR ME HERE. I SHALL NOT BE MORE THAN HALF AN HOUR.

AS THEY WAITED, ATHOS RESTLESSLY PACED BACK AND FORTH.

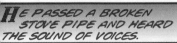

HE PASSED A BROKEN STOVE PIPE AND HEARD THE SOUND OF VOICES.

HUSH! THE CARDINAL IS SPEAKING TO SOMEONE IN THE CHAMBER ABOVE.

THE THREE MUSKETEERS GATHERED AROUND THE PIPE.

I HEAR A LADY'S VOICE.

WHAT DO YOU WISH, MONSEIGNEUR?

YOU ARE TO TELL THE DUKE OF BUCKINGHAM I HAVE PROOFS OF HIS MEETINGS WITH THE QUEEN, AND THAT I WILL REVEAL THEM IF HE CONTINUES WITH THIS WAR.

BUT IT IS POSSIBLE HE MAY PERSIST.

THEN A WAY WILL HAVE TO BE FOUND TO KILL HIM.

I WILL FIND THE WAY. BUT IN EXCHANGE FOR BUCKINGHAM, I WISH THE DEATH OF ONE OF MY ENEMIES.

WHAT IS HIS NAME?

D'ARTAGNAN.

VERY WELL. GIVE ME PAPER AND PEN.

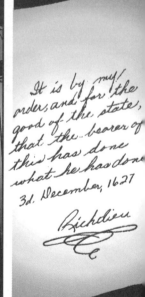

SOON...

It is by my orders, and for the good of the state, that the... bearer of this has done what he has done

3d. December, 1627

Richelieu

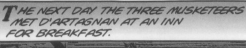
THE NEXT DAY THE THREE MUSKETEERS MET D'ARTAGNAN AT AN INN FOR BREAKFAST.

CONFOUND IT! THIS PLACE IS TOO NOISY FOR A PRIVATE CONFERENCE.

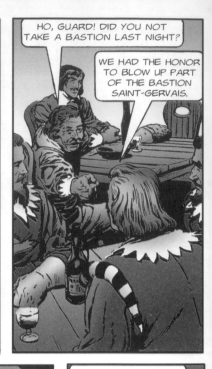
HO, GUARD! DID YOU NOT TAKE A BASTION LAST NIGHT?

WE HAD THE HONOR TO BLOW UP PART OF THE BASTION SAINT-GERVAIS.

IT IS PROBABLE THE ENEMY WILL SEND MEN TO REINSTATE IT THIS MORNING.

A WAGER, GENTLEMEN! I BET YOU THAT MY THREE FRIENDS AND I WILL GO AND BREAKFAST AT THE BASTION, AND THAT WE WILL STAY THERE AN HOUR, WHATEVER THE ENEMY MAY DO.

HE IS GOING TO GET US ALL KILLED.

NO. THIS WILL GIVE US A CHANCE TO TALK IN PRIVATE WITHOUT AROUSING SUSPICION.

THE FOUR MEN WERE SOON ESTABLISHED IN THE BASTION.

NOW, ATHOS, WHAT DID YOU WISH TO TELL ME?

I SAW MILADY YESTERDAY.

WHAT!

ATHOS RELATED WHAT HAD HAPPENED THE NIGHT BEFORE. SUDDENLY...

ABOUT 20 MEN ARE COMING TOWARD US.

THERE ARE ONLY FOUR SOLDIERS. THE REST ARE WORKMEN. I WILL WARN THEM AWAY.

GENTLEMEN, WE ARE BREAKFASTING. PLEASE WAIT UNTIL WE HAVE FINISHED, IF YOU HAVE BUSINESS HERE.

IN ANSWER, SEVERAL BULLETS FLATTENED THEMSELVES IN THE WALL AROUND ATHOS.

THE FOUR FRIENDS REPLIED WITH A VOLLEY THAT PUT THE GROUP TO FLIGHT.

THEN...

TO CONTINUE, MILADY MUST BE ON HER WAY TO ENGLAND. I THINK THE BEST THING TO DO WOULD BE TO WRITE TO LORD DE WINTER, HER BROTHER-IN-LAW, AND TELL HIM HER PLANS REGARDING BUCKINGHAM.

GENTLEMEN, TO ARMS! MORE TROOPS APPROACH.

FOUR SHOTS RANG OUT AND FOUR OF THE ENEMY FELL.

ALTHOUGH THE FOUR FRENCHMEN CONTINUED TO FIRE, A DOZEN SOLDIERS REACHED THE FOOT OF THE BASTION.

LET US FINISH THEM AT A BLOW. TO THE WALL!

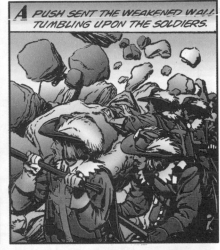

A PUSH SENT THE WEAKENED WALL TUMBLING UPON THE SOLDIERS.

I BELIEVE THAT FINISHES IT, GENTLEMEN. NOW, AS WE HAVE BEEN HERE AN HOUR, I SUGGEST WE RETURN TO OUR COMRADES.

BECAUSE OF HIS PART IN THIS ADVENTURE, D'ARTAGNAN WAS MADE A MUSKETEER.

THE DREAM OF MY LIFE HAS COME TRUE!.

THE FOUR MUSKETEERS SENT A LETTER TO LORD DE WINTER. WHEN MILADY ARRIVED IN ENGLAND, A YOUNG NAVAL OFFICER MET HER.

PLEASE COME WITH ME.

SHE WAS ESCORTED TO A CHATEAU AND LEFT IN A ROOM WITH BARRED WINDOWS.

I AM A PRISONER. WHAT DOES THIS MEAN?

THEN LORD DE WINTER APPEARED IN THE DOORWAY.

LEAVE US ALONE, MASTER FELTON.

I KNOW WHAT BRINGS YOU TO ENGLAND, BUT YOU SHALL NOT SUCCEED.

IN ONE WEEK I WILL HAVE AN ORDER OF DEPORTATION WHICH WILL PLACE YOU THOUSANDS OF MILES FROM ENGLAND. MEANWHILE, I HOPE YOU WILL BE COMFORTABLE HERE.

MONSTER!

WHEN DE WINTER LEFT, MILADY PACED UP AND DOWN IN A FURY.

THIS TOO I MUST OWE TO D'ARTAGNAN. FIRST THE AFFAIR OF THE STUDS, THEN MY BRAND AND NOW THIS. OH, REVENGE! REVENGE!

BUT IN ORDER TO AVENGE MYSELF I MUST BE FREE. PERHAPS I CAN WIN OVER THE YOUNG OFFICER WHO BROUGHT ME HERE. IT IS MY ONLY CHANCE.

FELTON, THE OFFICER, CAME TO OVERSEE HER WELFARE SEVERAL TIMES A DAY. AT EACH VISIT MILADY DID ALL SHE COULD TO WIN HIS SYMPATHY.

ARE YOU ILL, MILADY?

OH, HOW I HAVE SUFFERED!

IF YOU BUT KNEW MY STORY, YOU WOULD SEE THAT WHAT LORD DE WINTER TELLS YOU IS UNTRUE.

YOU HAVE BEEN WRONGED, THEN?

OH, YES, BY HIM, BUT EVEN MORE BY THE INFAMOUS DUKE OF BUCKINGHAM.

BY SKILLFUL LIES MILADY PERSUADED FELTON THAT SHE SHOULD BE FREED, AND THAT BUCKINGHAM SHOULD BE MURDERED. THE NIGHT BEFORE SHE WAS TO BE DEPORTED, SHE HEARD A TAP AT THE WINDOW.

FELTON! I AM SAVED!

YES, BUT BE SILENT. I MUST FILE THROUGH THESE BARS.

WHEN HE HAD FINISHED...

PUT YOUR ARMS AROUND MY NECK AND FEAR NOTHING.

SLOWLY THEY DESCENDED.

WHEN THEY REACHED THE BOTTOM, FELTON LED MILADY TO A DESERTED STRETCH OF COAST. THERE A SHIP WAITED.

THIS VESSEL WILL TAKE YOU WHEREVER YOU WANT TO GO.

BUT WHAT WILL YOU DO?

I MUST FIND BUCKINGHAM. HE IS DUE TO SAIL FOR LA ROCHELLE TOMORROW.

HE MUST NOT SAIL!

BE SATISFIED. HE WILL NOT!

MILADY RETURNED TO FRANCE AND WENT TO A CONVENT TO AWAIT FURTHER ORDERS FROM RICHELIEU.

AND FELTON SLEW THE DUKE OF BUCKINGHAM.

AH! TRAITOR! YOU HAVE KILLED ME.

AT THE CONVENT, MILADY MET ANOTHER YOUNG WOMAN.

AND WHY ARE YOU STAYING HERE, MY DEAR?

I WAS IN THE EMPLOY OF THE QUEEN, AND WHEN THE CARDINAL FOUND OUT ABOUT CERTAIN SERVICES I HAD DONE FOR HER, HE HAD ME ABDUCTED.

BUT THE QUEEN FOUND OUT WHERE I WAS AND HAD ME BROUGHT HERE FOR SAFETY.

YOU ARE CONSTANCE BONACIEUX!

YES, MILADY, BUT HOW DID YOU KNOW?

WE HAVE A MUTUAL FRIEND, MONSIEUR D'ARTAGNAN. HAVE YOU HAD ANY NEWS FROM HIM?

OH, YES. I HAVE JUST HAD A NOTE THAT HE IS COMING HERE FOR ME THIS VERY NIGHT!

SUDDENLY A CLATTER OF HOOFS WAS HEARD.

PERHAPS THAT IS D'ARTAGNAN. OH, MY HEART BEATS SO I CANNOT WALK!

SWIFTLY MILADY POURED A GLASS OF WINE AND SLIPPED A REDDISH POWDER INTO IT.

HERE, THIS WILL GIVE YOU STRENGTH.

CONSTANCE DRANK AND SANK TO THE GROUND, AS MILADY FLED.

THIS IS NOT THE WAY I WISHED TO AVENGE MYSELF, BUT WE DO WHAT WE CAN.

WHEN THE FOUR MUSKETEERS ARRIVED, CONSTANCE WAS DYING.

WHO DID THIS TO YOU?

SHE CALLED HERSELF... MILADY.

THIS MONSTER HAS LIVED TOO LONG! WAIT FOR ME HERE. I HAVE MEASURES TO TAKE.

*A*THOS RETURNED WITH A TALL MASKED MAN. THEY SET OUT AND FOUND MILADY AT A LONELY HOUSE.

WE WANT THE PERSON KNOWN AS MILADY DE WINTER--TO PUNISH HER FOR HER CRIMES.

OH, GOD! AND WHO IS THIS?

THE EXECUTIONER!

*T*HE EXECUTIONER LED MILADY TO A BOAT AT A NEARBY RIVER. WHEN HE ROWED HER TO THE OTHER SIDE, THE FOUR MUSKETEERS SAW HIS SWORD GLEAM AND THEN FALL.

GOD'S JUSTICE BE DONE. DIE IN PEACE.

THE FOUR MUSKETEERS RETURNED TO LA ROCHELLE. D'ARTAGNAN WAS ARRESTED AND BROUGHT BEFORE CARDINAL RICHELIEU.

YOU HAVE CONTINUALLY GIVEN ME TROUBLE, MONSIEUR-- IN THE AFFAIR OF THE STUDS AND NOW --

IT IS TRUE, AND ANOTHER MIGHT ANSWER YOU THAT HE HAS HIS PARDON IN HIS POCKET.

WHAT?

D'ARTAGNAN GAVE THE CARDINAL THE NOTE ATHOS HAD TAKEN FROM MILADY.

ALTHOUGH WE HAVE BEEN ENEMIES, SUCH COURAGE AS YOURS MUST BE REWARDED. HERE IS A LIEUTENANT'S COMMISSION IN THE MUSKETEERS.

D'ARTAGNAN IMMEDIATELY SOUGHT OUT HIS FRIENDS.

EACH OF YOU IS MORE WORTHY OF THIS COMMISSION THAN I.

KEEP IT, MY BOY. NO ONE DESERVES IT MORE.

SOON AFTER, PORTHOS LEFT THE MUSKETEERS TO MARRY A RICH WIDOW, ARAMIS ENTERED A MONASTERY AND ATHOS RETIRED TO THE COUNTRY. D'ARTAGNAN TOOK POSSESSION OF HIS RANK AND CONTINUED TO SERVE HIS KING.

THE END

THE THREE MUSKETEERS
ALEXANDRE DUMAS

The Three Musketeers was published in the middle of the 19th century to instant popularity. It has been translated into just about every language—there are numerous English translations—turned into a stage play, and in our century, there have been at least sixty different movie and TV versions. The adventures of the young, heroic d'Artagnan and his three noble friends, Athos, Porthos, and Aramis, are almost as well known world-wide as those of Robin Hood and King Arthur. Dumas wrote sequels, dealing with later events in d'Artagnan's life (*Twenty Years After*, and *Vicomte de Bragelonne*); some literary critics consider Dumas's great novel *The Count of Monte Cristo* to be his masterwork, but *The Three Musketeers* has remained his most well-loved.

It's often said that adventures are great to read about and terrible to live through. Most of us today would rather not have their lives threatened several times a day. The idea of confronting powerful political figures who can have one thrown into prison, or killed, is terrifying.

But it's great fun to live vicariously through heroic figures; not to care a snap of the fingers for the rich and powerful, to exchange witty comments before, during, and even after a duel-to-the-death. The four companions are swashbucklers at their very best: brave, loyal to one another, witty, courageous, and successful. They behave well toward those they love, and when they confront their enemies, they do it with style.

The Author

Born July 24, 1802, of a blended family of whom he was proud (his father was the son of the Marquis de la Pailleterie and Marie Cessette Dumas, a black woman from Santo Domingo), Alexandre Dumas was almost as dashing and charismatic a figure as his characters. His father was at first a common soldier, but rose through his brilliance and bravery to become a general in Napoleon's army. Unfortunately the father, who adopted the name Dumas, died in 1806, leaving his family to hard times.

Alexandre managed to get a job in the household of the Duke of Orleans, but his real efforts went into his attempts to write for the theatre. He made friends with many of the young poets and playwrights who later led the Romantic movement.

Dumas wrote quickly. Nowadays his plays would be regarded as overly melodramatic, but at the time they were enormously popular. *Henri et sa cour*, produced in 1829, was a sensationalistic story set during the French Renaissance. He wrote another bombastic play about Napoleon Bonaparte in 1831 that was just as popular, and in the same year he had another extravagant drama produced, called *Antony*.

Though he continued to write plays, Dumas turned his attention next to producing novels. He liked best writing action-packed historical novels set during the turbulent, colorful 16th or 17th centuries. He often collaborated with a writer named Auguste Maquet, who seems to have done much of the historical research and who contributed at least some of the plots. Today Maquet would probably get his name on the books; but at the time the full credit went to Dumas, and it's likely that the exciting pace, the witty dialogue and the character insight were Dumas's as well.

His great books —*The Three Musketeers*, and its sequels, and Dumas's masterpiece, *The Count of Monte Cristo*—were written largely in the period between 1840 and 1850, before political events led to revolution and a subsequent decline in public tastes for stories about kings and dukes.

Meanwhile, Dumas had become famous. He seemed to find it irresistible to try to live like his heroes, and Paris gossip of the time was full of stories of his practical jokes, extravagant gestures, duels, and love affairs. An Englishman named Captain Gronow, who is famous for his chatty memoires about famous people of London and Paris during the 19th Century, had this to say about Dumas:

"The sums which the 'Pere Prodigué [by this time Dumas's son, also named Alexandre, was also earning fame as a writer—he was usually called "Dumas *Fils*" (which means son in French)] spent on his Monte-Cristo villa...were fabulous. He was horribly cheated by architects, builders, upholsterers, and in fact by everybody he employed.

"Dumas is one of the most amusing men I ever met and a most wonderful talker. His wit is prodigious, his fund of anecdotes inexhaustible, and the strength of his lungs overpowering.... I was present at a dinner some twelve or fifteen years ago where Lord Brougham and Dumas were among the company, and the loquacious and eloquent ex-chancellor could not get in a single word, but had to sit, for the first time in his life, a perfect dummy."

Dumas loved fame and fortune, so much that unfortunately he spent a lot more than he earned. When he separated from his wife, he promised a handsome sum to support her, but he seldom paid it. When he found out that she was living in poverty, Dumas promptly promised to double the amount—but to this a friend said that he'd do better to pay the original allowance.

Dumas spent the last years of his life writing very hasty books which were not very successful, because he desperately needed money to pay his growing debts. He tried journalism, and writing other types of books such as travel volumes, but these were not successful. He died in 1870; his son went on to more modest fame, writing novels and plays about social problems and the sanctity of marriage and family.

The Classics Illustrated adaptation stays fairly close to the plot of *The Three Musketeers*. At the start, d'Artagnan, a brash, handsome young man of Gascony, leaves his home with his ridiculous yellow horse, his father's sword, and a letter of recommendation to Monsieur Treville, the captain of the Musketeers. At the town of Meung he gets into a fight with a mysterious figure (Rochefort) who is actually an agent of Cardinal Richelieu, sent to give orders to the beautiful Milady de Winter.

He makes his way to Paris and meets Monsieur de Treville, who assures him that only the king can pick his Musketeers—after several war campaigns, "certain brilliant actions, or at least two years' service in some other regiment less favored than ours." M. de Treville offers to enroll him him in the Royal Academy, where he will learn horsemanship, swordsmanship, and dancing—all necessities for being accepted as a gentleman. As he listens, D'Artagnan sees Rochefort out the window, and in his haste to get his revenge on the cardi-nal's agent he runs into—literally—the three Musketeers: Athos (noble in bearing, his manner indicating a sad secret); Porthos, gaudily dressed, and bragging always of his lovely duchess lady friend; and Aramis, thin and handsome and given to theological studies and to poetry. Aramis is softspoken and talks of wishing to withdraw to the church, but d'Artagnan later notes that he is very popular with highborn ladies. These three are Treville's bravest, most famous Musketeers—and each of the three challenge d'Artagnan to a duel. The four meet—and are challenged by the Cardinal's Guards, whom they defeat. Having acquitted himself with skill and courage, d'Artagnan is accepted as a friend by the three who had previously challenged him. After another encounter with the Cardinal's Guards, the King himself awards d'Artagnan forty pistoles, which enables the young Gascon to hire a servant and lodgings.

How does d'Artagnan ensure the

loyalty of his new servant? He is advised by the others: "This is a family affair. It is with valets as it is with wives, they must be placed at once upon the footing in which you wish them to remain." Therefore d'Artagnan thrashes Planchet, his servant, and then forbids him to leave his service. "For I look for better times. Your fortune is therefore made if you remain with me." Planchet is so impressed that he straightaway becomes d'Artagnan's loyal valet.

CAN THEY HAVE BEEN STOLEN?

THE ONLY TIME I WORE THESE STUDS WAS AT A BALL LAST WEEK. MILADY DE WINTER STOOD BESIDE ME TALKING FOR QUITE A LONG TIME.

All this leads into the Affair of the Diamonds. Bonacieux, the (unpaid) landlord of d'Artagnan's lodging, comes begging for help in locating his missing wife, who is seamstress to Queen Anne. Given money to find her, d'Artagnan promises help—but in trying to do so, he gets poor old Bonacieux arrested. Having set up the apartment as a trap, he rescues young, lovely Constance Bonacieux, and then as a favor to her, ends up escorting the Duke of Buckingham, who is secretly in Paris, to the palace for an interview with Queen Anne.

Buckingham is in love with the beautiful young queen, who—despite her feelings for the handsome duke—intends to stay loyal to the King, and to France. As a parting gift of friendship she gives Buckingham an expensive necklace of diamond studs. As she is always spied on, the missing necklace is reported to Cardinal Richelieu, who sees a way to destroy the Queen and strike at England through Buckingham. He sends Milady de Winter to steal two of the studs from the Duke, who has returned to England. The Cardinal, meanwhile, cleverly makes friends with poor, terrified Bonacieux and sets him to spy on his own wife, who the Cardinal knows is loyal only to the Queen. Then he gets the king to organize a big party—to which the queen is to wear her famous diamond necklace. If she cannot produce the necklace all will be lost!

The Queen sends Constance for help; *she* turns first to her husband, who threatens to tell the Cardinal, and then to d'Artagnan who, with the three Musketeers, promises to help. Bonacieux does warn the Cardinal—which makes the trip dangerous for the Musketeers. One by one they are waylaid, except for d'Artagnan, who makes it to England and meets the Duke of Buckingham. Angered—the Duke realizes that he has been tricked by Milady— Buckingham orders his craftsmen to replace the studs, and when that is done, he tries to reward d'Artagnan, who is offended. The young Gascon insists that what he has done has been in loyalty to the Queen, and not to Buckingham, who is English and therefore an enemy. Buckingham, delighted by his courage, sees to it that d'Artagnan is sped back to Paris on his errand.

The ball takes place; the studs are safely there, and when the king—perplexed at having two extra—turns to the Cardinal, Richelieu says suavely that he wished to present them to the

Queen—and does so through the King. Queen Anne grins, saying she is grateful, for "I am certain that these two studs alone have cost as much as all the others cost His Majesty." Later, in private, she rewards d'Artagnan with a beautiful diamond ring.

On their return to Paris, M. de Treville informs d'Artagnan that he is now a Musketeer, but they must all get ready to march off to war, as the campaign is to begin the first of May. In those days, men had to provide their own uniforms, weapons, horses, and equipment—and they were all anxious to appear as gentlemen.

D'Artagnan plans to meet Constance (with whom he is enamored!), but she again disappears mysteriously. He then has to go back and retrieve his three friends from the places they fell, and the story of their recovery, and how they get their money (and the duels they fight) is a comedy of errors and misunderstandings. In the midst of it, Athos tells d'Artagnan the sad story of his former great titles and wealth, and the beautiful young woman he had married who turned out to be a thief. His honor disgraced, Athos tried to hang her, gave up everything, and took on the persona of "Athos."

While Porthos tries to trick his money out of his "duchess" (his bourgeois lady friend) and Aramis gets his from one of his many aristocratic lady friends, d'Artagnan is lured into meeting the beautiful but devious Milady, who is thirsting for revenge against d'Artagnan for the affair of the diamonds, and for thwarting her in another affair on which he stumbled accidently. Her manner of revenge is to make friends with him and set up a flirtation. Unfortunately for her, he also makes friends with her maid, Kitty, whom he sees Milady mistreating. Through Kitty he finds out just how wicked Milady is—and even overhears Milady telling Kitty just how she's going to trick him and kill him. He tricks her instead; she grabs

Returning together, d'Artagnan and his friends fight a duel with some Englishmen, one of whom turns out to be M. de Winter—Milady's husband.

his sword and tries to kill him, and in the struggle he uncovers her shoulder and sees the brand of the fleur-de-lis on her skin, which means that she was once convicted of being a thief. He now knows she is Athos's wicked wife, not dead—but alive, and more wicked than ever.

The last third of the book takes place when the Musketeers are on campaign in the south. They are to attack the Huguenot fortress at La Rochelle, which is to be aided by the English under the Duke of Buckingham. They encounter Cardinal Richelieu, who is going to meet Milady; she obtains an open letter of pardon, which she plans to use after she contrives the murder of d'Artagnan. Athos gets the letter from her.

A WAGER, GENTLEMEN! I BET YOU THAT MY THREE FRIENDS AND I WILL GO AND BREAKFAST AT THE BASTION, AND THAT WE WILL STAY THERE AN HOUR, WHATEVER THE ENEMY MAY DO.

Later, when the four Musketeers need to talk without being overheard by other soldiers in the camp, they make a bet with other soldiers that they will breakfast on the bastion. As the whole camp turns out to watch them, they eat, discuss Milady and the Cardinal, and twice fight off the enemy, each time winning by cleverness and courage. The Cardinal, watching all this from a distance, knows that d'Artagnan is the kind of man he wants as his own.

Milady is sent to England to get rid of Buckingham. Her husband imprisons her, but she escapes after winning his trusted lieutenant, Felton, to her side. She talks Felton into assassinating Buckingham, then makes her way back to France, to put into action her plans for revenge against d'Artagnan. She means to lure him to the place where she is keeping Constance Bonacieux. The Musketeers arrive to rescue Constance, who is poisoned by Milady. Angered, they corner her, serve as judge and tribunal, and execute her.

When the Cardinal summons d'Artagnan and seems about to have him thrown in prison for his actions, the young man produces the very letter Richelieu wrote for Milady, pardoning the bearer. The Cardinal is impressed, and offers d'Artagnan a lieutenancy in the guards. The young man tries to offer it to each of his three friends,

THE EXECUTIONER LED MILADY TO A BOAT AT A NEARBY RIVER. WHEN HE ROWED HER TO THE OTHER SIDE, THE FOUR MUSKETEERS SAW HIS SWORD GLEAM AND THEN FALL.

GOD'S JUSTICE BE DONE. DIE IN PEACE.

but they refuse: Athos wants to retire, Porthos is going to marry his "duchess," whose old husband recently died, and Aramis is going into the church at last. They celebrate; later, d'Artagnan and Rochefort fight three duels, then make friends before they can fight a fourth. Bonacieux, who cared little what happened to his wife, tries to get to the Cardinal to pay for his spying—and disappears.

The Real Musketeer

D'Artagnan was a real person, born around 1620. He was the captain of the King's Musketeers for many long years; he died at the seige of Maastricht in 1673. He is mentioned several times by no less a personage than Louis XIV—specifically in reference to the arrest of the minister Fouquet, a plot devised by the young king himself. There are numerous mentions of him in connection with this arrest in the letters of Madame de Sevigny, in which d'Artagnan comes across as a humane, honest man.

Queen Anne was Spanish by birth, a descendent of the imperial Hapsburgs who ruled the Holy Roman Empire. Her brother, Philip IV, ruled Spain. She was just a teenager when she was married to Louis XIII: a beautiful, intelligent young woman who enjoyed court life. She was disliked and distrusted by many at court (notably the king and his chief counsellor, Cardinal Richelieu) mostly because she wrote letters to her brother in Spain—they always assumed she was plotting against the French. They also resented her because it took nearly twenty years for her to produce an heir to the kingdom. That this was mainly Louis XIII's fault, no one considered. It was common to blame the woman if there was no child, *or* the child was a girl, *or* didn't live; Anne apparently lived most of those twenty years in fear she would be sent back to Spain in disgrace for failing to provide France with an heir. Her life at court was not very happy; she was largely ignored, and thus ripe for beguiling by the handsome, dashing Duke of Buckingham when he visited Paris. Their friendship only made the king more suspicious, and gave Richelieu another excuse to spy on her, which he did until his death.

Louis XIII was a sickly, weak man who was timid and afraid of women, including his own wife—which is the main reason it took twenty years to produce a son. There is not much to say about his work as a king, because he was guided in everything by the powerful Cardinal Richelieu.

Cardinal Richelieu is a fascinating figure. Born Armand-Jean du Plessis, later Duc de Richelieu, he was a complex man who became the single most important figure in French government during the first half of the 1600s. He was a pale, sickly boy who showed tremendous ability in studies and debate. His father had been provost to King Henry III, but died leaving the family estates impoverished. Armand-Jean was a third son, destined for the church as a bishop. Despite his youth, and some initial hostile resistance, he did such a good job he later found himself in Paris, as chaplain to the Queen Mother. The king, Henry IV, was assassinated in

1610, leaving a son (Louis XIII) who was still a child, under a regency government guided by the Queen Mother, Marie de Medici. Terrible political brangles ensued for the next twenty years, and when the king and Richelieu emerged victorious, the king was suspicious of everyone (including his wife and brother) and Richelieu had become a master of politics. From that time, his goal was to build a strong central government in France with the King at its head, so that the nobles could no longer tear the country to pieces seeking for power. He died in 1642, having just foiled a plot against his life led by one of Louis XIII's favorites.

The Duke of Buckingham led a kind of storybook life. He was born George Villiers, son of a knight. He was handsome, charismatic, and smart—but, disastrously, unschooled in statecraft. When he was introduced to the King of England, James I, in 1614, the King was delighted with the clever, dashing young man. Honors and titles were piled on him as the years went by; he was made a duke in 1623, and became a close friend of Charles, the crown prince. When James died in 1625, Charles took the throne, and Buckingham became the most important man in England. He arranged the king's marriage with the French princess Henrietta Maria, which angered many English; he also sent an invasionary force against Spain, which was so badly organized they had to turn back before they got to Cadiz, their intended point of attack. Buckingham sent soldiers to aid the French Protestants at New Rochelle (referred to in the book); he stayed with his forces four months, showing great personal courage but a total lack of training or experience in commanding an army. His forces were shattered, and he returned home. Despite Parliament's angry insistence that the king get rid of Buckingham, the Duke planned to raise another force—but he was assassinated by John Felton, a naval lieutenant who had fought in Buckingham's disastrous campaigns, and who mistakenly thought he was carrying out the wishes of the members of Parliament.

Historical Content

The best introduction to the setting of *The Three Musketeers* ought to come from the author himself. The story opens in April, 1626:

In those times panics were common, and few days passed without some city or other enregistering in its archives an event of this kind. There were nobles, who made war against each other; there was the king, who made war against the cardinal; there was Spain, which made war against the king. Then, in addition to these concealed or public, secret or open wars, there were robbers, mendicants, Huguenots, wolves, and scoundrels, who made war upon everybody. The citizens always took up arms readily against thieves, wolves, or scoundrels, often against nobles or Huguenots, sometimes against the king, but never against the cardinal or Spain.

Who are all these combatants? Robbers, wolves, and scoundrels are easy enough; mendicants are beggars,

Men and Women

In 1626, standards for behavior for men and women were very different: women were expected to behave according to their status, and to live circumspectly. Men—husbands, brothers, fathers—were expected to protect their women's honor. A woman didn't do much more than what was expected of her: she could be blamed and attacked for doing the sorts of things that men did. So, for example, d'Artagnan could languish after Constance Bonacieux without blame; she, however, had to be very careful lest her reputation be ruined.

Still, it's hard to blame Constance for *wanting* a flirtation! Marriages were usually arranged by parents, and it was common for a girl of 16 or 18 to be married to a man of 50; men married later, for they had to earn enough to support a family. A father might cement a business partnership by marrying his daughter to a colleague. Once a person was married, for whatever reason, it was for life. Divorce was very rare. Also, people who devoted themselves to religious lives were forbidden to marry. Everyone knew these rules, but people often bent them—men especially. Aristrocratic women had a bit more freedom, but women who bent the rules took greater risks than men. Young wives sometimes fell in love with someone closer to their age—as Constance did with the handsome, dashing d'Artagnan. But if there was a problem, inevitably it was the woman who was punished, even ruined for life.

In a society where your status was dictated by birth, it was also a given that once you had been imprisoned for a crime, the rest of your life you were regarded by everyone as a criminal. Again, this was especially harsh for women. Note, in the book, that the Musketeers think the story of Porthos's servant Mousqueton and his thievery funny and clever—but they are horrified and disgusted when they find out that Athos's wife (Milady de Winter) had been branded once for stealing…even though there is no evidence in the book that she did anything wrong *after* she married Athos. In fact, they think it appropriate that Athos, on finding the brand on her shoulder, promptly tried to hang her!

---

or homeless people. "Spain" means the king of Spain, Philip IV. Huguenots are French Protestants.

A Warlike Society

In those days, gentlemen went about armed with at least a sword, often a knife or two as well. Peasants were not permitted to carry swords—they were considered the weapons of soldiers or gentlemen of "good birth"—but they often had their own weapons for the protection of family and village, since no one else really looked out for them. Robbers and homeless brigands attacked sporadically, and during the spring and summer was the war season, which the nobles and their regiments might chase back and forth across the land in their seemingly unending battles. No one complained, for this was what life had been like for centuries, and everyone thought it would be that way for ever. Many, in fact, were afraid of change: the religious wars were proof that change could be deadly.

Religion and War

These days, we're used to religious freedom. Your neighbors might practice one religion, and the people across the street a completely different one—or they might not be religious at all—but for the most part no one cares, and this causes no problems.

But for centuries—over a thousand years—there was only one religion practiced by everyone in Europe, Roman Catholicism. People believed that the universe was organized in a kind of ladder, with God at the top, followed by heavenly denizens, then the planets in order (everything circling around Earth), and then King and Pope, nobles and higher clergy, knights and lower clergy, and peasants at the bottom—just above animals. Everyone knew their place, and dressed according to their status. You knew at a glance what class each person belonged to; though everyone wanted to move up in status, it happened rarely, and mostly through force of arms (or, for women, through marriage).

Then, in the 1500s, the Protestant movement was born. "Protestant" comes from "Protest"—the Protestants believed in much the same doctrine but believed the Church needed to be reorganized and reformed. The idea of two churches

frightened many: devout Catholics believed that Protestants would go to hell, or that God would punish everyone with earthquakes and plagues and flood and famine if the old ways were not followed. Rulers had an additional worry—as Protestants banded together, it became apparent that their reforms might not be limited to the church. As rulers became Protestant, political tensions grew. Terrible religious wars ripped across Europe during the 1500s and 1600s.

Class, Combat, and the Musketeers

To understand the peculiar situation of d'Artagnan and his friends it's necessary to go back almost a millenium, to the chaotic years after the collapse of the Roman Empire in the 5th century, when Europe was crossed every which way by marauding raiders—Goths, Ostrogoths, Visigoths, Vikings, Huns, and countless others. The manor system developed during these rough years. Warriors, who trained for one job alone, defended the manor—or castle. Because the warriors were busy training in arms, the jobs of building, growing the food, making cloth and furniture and work implements were done by peasants. The lord of the castle promised to protect the peasants; in turn his warriors would be provided with the necessities of life. Good enough, in theory.

As the centuries went by, raids from outside were fewer, but the system remained the same. Peasants were expected to deliver goods and or money on specific "rent" days, regardless of whether they were being protected or not. Lords *liked* being lords—commanding a great castle, dressing in fine clothes, and being entertained through winters by players and minstrels. When the spring thaws came, though, if there wasn't a threat from raiders, the lords and their soldiers would go looking for trouble. Kings had trouble with barons who wanted more land and more power; barons rebelled against kings they thought were poor leaders.

The most successful kings, of course, were those who were brilliant at war.

Brilliant or not, the lords—nobles, now—by now believed that it was beneath them to do any job *but* fight. Which meant smart kings found *some* reason to lead restless nobles into battle—or send rebellious ones to war. This was the Age of Chivalry; but there was one constant that court

Servants

In the 17th century, personal honor required that you live as ostentatiously as possible. This required, for those of upper classes, great houses maintained by armies of servants.

When we think of servants, the image may be of crisply uniformed maids, footmen, and butlers performing meticulously outlined chores, then whisking themselves out of sight of their aristocratic employers, who scarcely take notice of them. This cold, correct behaviour is again the opposite of the 17th century.

Servant pay was bad— *when* they even received it, for there was no one to see to it that they were treated fairly. Too often they were employed by social superiors who were almost as poor as they. Therefore servants, like soldiers, frequently got their livings in the streets. Servants behaved toward their employers with a great deal of freedom; presuming their treatment wasn't so bad they ran away after being hired, they became like members of the family. Great dukes and princes thought nothing of playing chess with their servants; as we see in the book, visiting English aristocrats were perfectly willing to hazard games of chance with underlings.

SOON AFTER, THE FOUR FRIENDS LEFT PARIS ON A CAMPAIGN AGAINST THE ENGLISH AT LA ROCHELLE. D'ARTAGNAN, BEING IN ANOTHER COMPANY, WAS SEPARATED FROM THE THREE MUSKETEERS. ONE DAY—

WINE, MONSIEUR--A PRESENT FROM MESSIEURS ATHOS, PORTHOS AND ARAMIS.

Lackeys with little to do often cruised the streets of Paris, their livery lending them their employer's prestige, and often dukes and marquises would end up embroiled in street battles involving their servants. These aristocrats didn't think themselves above the squabbles of their servants. They could get quite fierce in protecting their own. Often enough—as we see in *The Three Musketeers*—servants and masters connived together to make a living in imaginative, if questionable, ways.

If nobody protected servants, they could, and did, protect themselves. It's true that aristocrats often beat their servants, but sometimes—as happened to the Princess d'Harcourt, a real woman at the French court about this time—the servants fought back. This haughty Princess was so harsh she couldn't keep maids for long. She had recently engaged a new maid, a strong young country girl who, when the Princess began beating her for some minor infraction, knocked the Princess down and gave her a good drubbing. When whispers about this got about the court, the Princess couldn't retaliate, but had to pretend it had never happened lest her prestige suffer permanently.

heralds and song-writers paid little attention to, and that was that the peasants were usually the ones who were the worst off—no matter whose side won.

By the 1600s, when *The Three Musketeers* is set, the days of the distant raiders were largely forgotten, but the system was still in place. Nobles still collected their rents, and peasants owned little or nothing, performed unending work, and were scorned by everyone in the classes above them.

What grew slowly in the centuries of peace was an in-between layer of people, the ones Dumas calls the "Bourgeoisie." These are the shopkeepers and traders, the business people of the time—the ones later that would be called "the middle class." They mostly lived in cities, and they did their best to rise in status even as the nobles scorned them.

Social pressure is still one of the slowest things to change. Though there was no longer the need for protection of centuries before, the nobles still couldn't do any kind of work but fighting. Especially in France, to engage in trade was to lose social status—prestige. If they were poor, nobles lived in their great, crumbling castles, and if they had money (or thought they could get some by courting the rulers' favor) they followed the royal court from castle to castle. Thus we see minor nobles such as our heroes living almost hand to mouth. Young noble men, especial-

ly younger sons, would go forth to seek their fortunes—and their choice of careers was pretty much limited to war. Thus, the Musketeers.

The King's Musketeers and the King's Army

The Musketeers were a kind of palace guard—an elite palace guard. Muskets had come into use some sixty years before this story takes place; they were the latest weapon, and the guards were the equivalent of today's elite fighting forces. They trained constantly (whether in drills or in street brawls when they had nothing else to do but roam around looking for fights) and they had the "high-tech" weaponry. When on duty, Musketeers guarded the royal palaces—but if the King wanted them to go to war, they did. When they were off-duty, they were free to do what they wanted, which often meant getting food, clothing and shelter in ways that did not involve *working* for a living. In Chapter Two, Dumas says: "Treville [captain of the Musketeers] understood admirably the war method of that period, in which he who could not live at the expense of his enemy must live at the expense of his compatriots."

When we think of life in the army, most of us remember television and movie depictions of spit-and-polish rows of soldiers in identical (government-supplied) uniforms, marching or doing pushups or deploying efficiently with megaweapons. In most movies they don't attack civilians on their own side, and they mostly avoid non-comabatant civilians on the other side. Camps are scrupulously tidy, they have a seemingly unending supply of weapons, and there is always plenty of food—it just doesn't taste very good.

Army life during the 16th century couldn't have been more different. War had been more or less constant for the past few hundred years. Kings were supposed to be warrior leaders; indeed, war was often called the sport

of kings. And many kings did ride with their soldiers.

This doesn't mean that the King was in control. The King was more of a top shareholder—and some of the regiments weren't at all his property. During King Louis XIII's reign, the main conflicts were with Spain, or at home with the Huguenots. The army was largely a nearly lawless rabble of hard-bitten men who fought hard and treated others harshly. They lived by extortion and looting, for their pay seldom reached their pockets (having been siphoned off by those above them—*if* it was issued!) Civilians on both sides were terrified when the soldiers marched through the area.

When the looting was so bad that even the soldiers' own officers were

robbed there were mass hangings. The rest of the time there wasn't much discipline—and the officers were usually as bad as their troops.

Officers were rarely promoted (which is why the Cardinal's offer to d'Artagnan is a big deal). Captains bought their regiments or companies. The state was *supposed* to provide pay for the soldiers (which sometimes happened and sometimes didn't). The captain would get a specific amount for each man, and in turn he was to train and equip them. The system was almost an invitation to fraud: captains often would hire a few homeless people, or put a weapon in the hands of a servant, to fill out their numbers for the *passe volant*—the parade in front of the commissioner. The captain would (theoretically) receive money for a hundred men, of whom maybe forty were "extras" who were paid to be soldiers for one day. The captain would pocket the sums for the invisible forty—and after the next battle, would report those forty as casualties (which, incidentally, makes the historical record of killed and wounded from the time highly suspect). Some captains would pocket *all* the money—but usually the captain's men, on finding that out, would desert as a group. Most of the time the captains cheated their men, just as they were cheated of the full sums by the commissioners and officers above them. This left the men to

• Take a look at the relationship between servant and master, focusing on Athos, Porthos, Aramis, d'Artagnan, Milady, and Monsieur de Winter (and Felton). How did these characters treat their servants, and what does this treatment tell you about their personalities and attitudes toward other people?

• Look at Athos's history of his marriage. Do you think Milady de Winter was treated fairly? Does this change your opinion of her? Can you write an alternate version of the story from her point of view?

• Give a character sketch of each of the four main characters, focusing on their actions and attitudes in two or three specific incidents. Which man do you think the most admirable by today's standards? Who is the least?

• Find and describe at least five customs in the book that everyone seems to practice, but which are no longer practiced today. Why do you think these came about—and why do you think they have changed?

• D'Artagnan seems to take great pride in his impulsiveness—even though it often gets him into a lot of trouble. What about his temper and impulsiveness seems valuable to you? Would this trait be valuable in today's world?

About the Essayist:

Sherwood Smith holds an M.A. from U.C. Santa Barbara; she is the author of numerous adult and young adult fantasy and science fiction books, including *Wren's War* (HBJ '95), and *Rifter's Covenant* (Tor '95). Ms. Smith teaches at Carden Conservatory.

get food and find their equipment any way they could. Which was, if there was no convenient enemy to loot, from the civilians they were meant to protect.

Soldiers were poorly trained. Their equipment—weapons and armor—was haphazardly obtained and maintained. Food, if supplied, was often rotten or shorted by speculating contractors. War camps, especially semi-permanent ones, were disgusting places: this was long before people recognized that unsanitary conditions led to disease. Sometimes, during especially hot summer campaigns, more men died of sickness than in battle.

Glory, Panache, Rep

So why be a Musketeer? In a sense, because it beat working for a living. Personal honor was at least as important as life to nobly born people. The higher the social status of the person, the more important it was to maintain one's honor. Kings had to fulfill their *gloire*, which is kind of a combination of honor and glory; everyone from royalty down worked hard to at least appear to live up to their status. Thus we see Porthos pretending to be better dressed than he is, or spending what

I CONFESS, YOUR GRACE, THAT WITH WAR IMMINENT BETWEEN OUR TWO COUNTRIES, I MUST LOOK UPON YOU AS A FUTURE ENEMY. THAT WHICH I DID, I DID FOR MY QUEEN.

IT IS NOT YOU WHO CAN GIVE ME LESSONS IN GOOD MANNERS, I WARN YOU.

little money he has on his appearance rather than food—even when he doesn't know where his next meal was coming from.

The other part of personal honor, for men, was courage (or its appearance). Men from Gascony (like d'Artagnan) were reputed to be courageous and daring—and of course many Gascons worked hard to live up to this reputation. Duels to the death could be, and were, fought over scornful looks, or being jostled when walking. Insults could be deadly. One was expected to behave to one's equals with politeness and courage; this courtesy did *not* extend to one's social inferiors. So we have d'Artagnan nobly refusing a reward from the hands Buckingham, his enemy (and his social better). At the same time, no one thinks anything of Porthos' attempts to swindle his bourgeoisie lady friend's husband out of as much money as he could get. The same with d'Artagnan's taking his landlord's money and then not bothering to execute the favor the man had asked—then, later, starting a flirtation with his wife.